PATRICIA C. McKISSACK

A MILLION FISH
...more or less

Illustrated by
DENA SCHUTZER

ALFRED A. KNOPF
New York

THIS IS A BORZOI BOOK PUBLISHED BY ALFRED A. KNOPF

Text copyright © 1992 by Patricia C. McKissack
Jacket art and interior illustrations copyright © 1992 by Dena Schutzer

Visit us on the Web! randomhousekids.com

Educators and librarians, for a variety of teaching tools, visit us at RHTeachersLibrarians.com

The Library of Congress has cataloged this work as follows:
McKissack, Pat.
A million fish . . . more or less / by Patricia C. McKissack ; illustrated by Dena Schutzer.
p. cm.
Summary: A boy learns that the truth is often stretched on the Bayou Clapateaux, and gets the chance to tell his own
version of a bayou tale when he goes fishing.
ISBN 978-0-679-80692-9 (trade) — ISBN 978-0-679-90692-6 (lib. bdg.) — ISBN 978-0-679-88086-8 (pbk.)
[1. Fishing—Fiction. 2. Tall tales.] I. Schutzer, Dena, ill. II. Title.
PZ7.M478693Mg 1991 [E]—dc20 90034322

MANUFACTURED IN CHINA
June 2016
15 14 13 12 11 10 9 8 7 6

To my sister, Sarah Frances Stuart,
and the real Hugh Thomas

—P. C. M.

To Emma and Ralph

—D. S.

It was early morning on the Bayou Clapateaux. Hugh Thomas had just tossed his line into the water when Papa-Daddy and Elder Abbajon came rowing out of the gauzy river fog. They were swapping bayou tales, just like they had for years.

"Morning to you," Hugh Thomas called as they pulled up alongside the bank.

Papa-Daddy started right in. "The Elder and me was just sayin' that the Bayou Clapateaux is a mighty peculiar place."

"Take the time back in '03, me and the Elder here caught a wild turkey weighed five hundred pounds!"

Hugh Thomas's eyes filled with wonder. "That's a powerful big turkey."

Quickly Elder Abbajon took up the story, adding,
"As we was marchin' that gobbler home,
I spied a lantern that'd been left by Spanish
conquistadores back in the year 15 and 42.
And it was still burning!"

"After three hundred and fifty years!"
Hugh Thomas exclaimed
in amazement.

Papa-Daddy lowered his voice to
a whisper. "Just when the Elder
picked up that lantern, the
ground commenced to
quaking, and the longest,
meanest cottonmouth
I ever
did see
raised up.

The thing had legs, and went to chasing us. The hounds broke and run, I got tangled up in the ropes, and that turkey got clean away.''

With a quick nod, he gave the story back to Elder Abbajon. '' 'Bout that time, a swarm of giant mosquitoes attacked. I lost my footin' and dropped the lantern in a pool of quicksand. Might' near fell in myself. 'Course, as you can see, I didn't then, 'cause I'm here now.''

Hugh Thomas studied on what the two ol' swampers had told him. Then he smiled. "Y'all are just funning—right?…Did that turkey *really* weigh five hundred pounds?"

"More or less," Papa-Daddy answered, snapping his suspenders and winking his eye.

"And was that lantern *really* over three hundred and fifty years old?"

"Give or take a year or two," Elder Abbajon answered, swattin' a mosquito.

"Was it *really* still burning?"

"Well, let's just say it was flickering a bit."

And with their tale all told, the two men rowed away.

"Remember," Papa-Daddy called just 'fore they disappeared behind the curtain of fog. "Strange things do happen on the Bayou Clapateaux."

Now Hugh Thomas was
alone with only worrisome mosquitoes to keep him company. But
it wasn't long before he caught three small fish.

And in the next half-hour he caught a *million* more! Big ones, little ones, all sizes. The boy was so excited he whooped with joy. "Wait 'til Papa-Daddy and Elder Abbajon see this!"

Then, loading his magnificent catch on his wagon, he turned to leave.

But without warning, two yellow eyes surfaced just above the water line. Hugh Thomas knew it was Atoo, the *grand-père* of all the alligators on Jackson's Pointe. The old gator slithered onto the bank, blocking the boy's way.

"Where do you think you will go with all our fish?" he hissed angrily.

Hugh Thomas blinked. Why, that gator was talking right out! "Th-th-these are my fish," the boy answered with an uncertain spirit.

Atoo's mean eyes took in the catch. "And what's for me and mine to eat if I let you take them all?"

Hugh Thomas considered making a run for it. But the old gator must have read his mind. "Don't even think of it," he warned, inching closer. Then he chuckled softly. "Your best chance is to figure on this. If one hundred alligators one hundred feet long can move at one hundred yards per second, how long would it take us to get from this water to you and your wagon of fish? Answer now," he hissed, moving still closer.

Not long enough for me to get away! Hugh Thomas thought. Deciding that anything was better than tangling with Atoo and all his kin, he solved the riddle by throwing a goodly amount of fish back into the bayou.

"You make the right answer," Atoo said. Then he turned and disappeared beneath the dark waters, along with the hundred other alligators who had been watching and waiting.

Hugh Thomas took a quick count, and saw he still had close to a half-million fish left. He followed the swamp path that was the quickest way to Papa-Daddy and Elder Abbajon's houseboat. Story had it that Jean Polet's pirate treasure was hidden somewhere 'mongst the cypress knees, but Hugh Thomas wasn't interested. "I've got my own treasure," he boasted.

The air grew thick, hovering over the swamp like a big smothering hand. Then the still came, a terrible kind of silence with its own sound. The boy hummed and quickened his step. Something was stalking him, closing in fast. The ghost of Jean Polet, maybe?

No! Hugh Thomas was suddenly surrounded by an army of raccoons, led by the most notorious rogue of them all—Mosley!

"By my leave!" shouted the bandit leader. "We'll be demanding a toll, li'l sir. And ye wagon of fish there will do nicely."

"Wait," Hugh Thomas cried out. "That's not fair!"

"Not fair, says he!" Mosley scoffed. "And what'll be fair to you?"

"Half, maybe?" Hugh Thomas couldn't believe he was bargaining with a band of pirate raccoons.

"Why settle on half, mate, when we can *take* it all?"

Thinking fast, Hugh Thomas suggested, "A contest? That's it! We'll have a contest of some kind."

Mosley laughed coarsely. "A contest it'll be. You win, we takes half the catch. I win, we takes it all. Mind you, that's as fair as it'll be gettin'."

The boy agreed, not knowing what to expect—swords, pistols, wrestling?

Then, to his astonishment, Mosley whistled, and two black bears appeared. Reaching beneath a huge swamp cabbage, the pirate pulled out a twenty-foot snake.
"We'll skip rope, says I!"
And so the contest began.

The bears turned and
Mosley jumped.

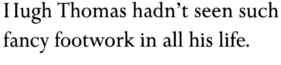

Hugh Thomas hadn't seen such
fancy footwork in all his life.

That rascal skipped so hard and so fast he was down in a pit when he finally missed on jump 5,552. His motley crew sent up a loud cheer.

But Hugh Thomas held his own—1,000...2,000...3,000... 4,000...4,050. Hugh Thomas jumped and jumped...5,000. He was so tired. His legs hurt, but he jumped some more...5,550. He managed just three more jumps before missing, but it was enough to win...5,553!

Mosley was purely outdone. He went to grumbling and mumbling and swearing under his breath. But in the end he made good his word. "I takes me lickin', and now I'll be takin' me fish."

One by one, hundreds of masked bandits marched past the wagon and plucked a juicy treat. Then Mosley found the plumpest fish for himself and beckoned Hugh Thomas to hurry along.

Even though his catch was cut by half again,
Hugh Thomas still felt like a winner. Moving with purpose,
he passed the large cypress stump called Napoleon's Elbow, then
quit the swamp. Winding his way through the deserted grounds of
the Mossland Mansion, he held with tradition and threw part
of his catch to the waterfowl that lived in the old garden pool.
Since slavery times, fishermen believed that feeding these
birds would bring them luck the next time out.

Thief! Thief! A fish crow spied Hugh Thomas's catch and sent up a signal. Birds darkened the sky. They swooped down, speared their fish, and soared away, screeching, *Thief! Thief!*

"Shoo!" shouted Hugh Thomas. But the birds chased him across the parish road and under the trestle, stopping just short of the first house in Free Jack's Quarters.

Chantilly, the neighbor girl's cat, was sunning on the porch steps. Her gray eyes were fixed on the wagonful of plump fish.

"Why, it's a Christmas gift!" the cat shouted, excitement swelling her words. "...To see you, that is," she added in a soft purr.

Hugh Thomas was surprised that the cat was talking, and to him. Most of the time, Chantilly wouldn't even look in his direction.

"It's not my custom to report on my mistress's whereabouts. But if you want to see Miss Challie Pearl, she's with Walter Edward, out back in the okra patch. Can't you hear them laughing together?"

Without thinking, Hugh Thomas hopped the fence and disappeared around the house.

Sometime later, he came back with his friend in tow. He was talking all excited and explaining. "Come see for yo'self. It was a million fish!"

Challie Pearl stopped. "What million? I see three little fish."

Hugh Thomas was completely confused. Then he looked at Chantilly and understood. "You tricked me," he accused her. "You ate my fish! Say you did!"

The cat blinked innocently and cleaned her whiskers. Challie Pearl scooped up her pet. "You must be addled, Hugh Thomas! Come tellin' that whopper, then layin' blame on my poor, precious kitty-cat." And she marched away in a huff.

Meanwhile a chorus of Chantilly's friends meowed contentedly as they licked their paws.

With only the three fish left, Hugh Thomas followed the
path to the backwater slough where Papa-Daddy and Elder
Abbajon's houseboat was tied up. They were sitting
on the front porch playing checkers.

"Seems the bayou let you come 'way with a
fine catch this morning," Elder Abbajon
said, smiling.

"Best luck a fisherman can have is to catch
just enough for dinner," Papa-Daddy put in.

"But I caught a million more,"
the boy boasted. "What happened
to 'em is a long story."

Papa-Daddy pulled his straw hat down over his eyes. Elder Abbajon leaned back in the old cane chair. And both of them propped their feet up on the railing. "So, you've learned that the Bayou Clapateaux is a mighty strange place."

"Tell us, now, was it *really* a million?"
A smile broke across Hugh Thomas's face, and he winked his eye.
"More or less," he answered, and started right in on his tale.